The Aqua Adventure

Words by Carrie Hasler   Pictures by Scott Soeder

Blue Sneaker Press

–For James and Cate–the best squad I could ever ask for. –CH

–For my family–I'd surely be lost without you. –SS

Story by Carrie Hasler
Illustrations by Scott Soeder

Coop Squad: The Aqua Adventure was published by Blue Sneaker Press.
Blue Sneaker works with authors, illustrators, nonprofit organizations,
and corporations to publish children's books that engage, entertain, and
educate kids on subjects that affect our world. Blue Sneaker Press is
an imprint of Southwestern Publishing Group, Inc.; 2451 Atrium Way,
Nashville, TN 37214. Southwestern Fundraising and Southwestern
Publishing Group are members of Southwestern Family of Companies.

With grateful appreciation to the following members of the
Southwestern Fundraising team: Brent Carter, Thomas Hixson,
Aaron Lynn, and Chris Rubel.

ISBN: 978-1-943198-07-8
Library of Congress Control Number: 2019936348
Printed in the United States
10 9 8 7 6 5 4 3 2 1

The typefaces used in this book are New Century Schoolbook and Bang
Whack Pow. The illustrations were drawn digitally in Adobe Photoshop.

Cover art and book design by Scott Soeder

It all started when Coop and Pork Chop had a bit of a bumpy landing. They had just returned home from Planet Gallus to find that the farm wasn't quite the same as when they had left it.

They didn't mean to land on Ted. You could say
it was a bit of a *crush* landing.

With a sigh of relief, Coop and Pork Chop joined Frankie at the campfire.

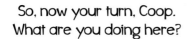

So, now your turn, Coop. What are you doing here?

Well, it started when I was just an itty-bitty egg here on the farm...

It was finally time for me to hatch. Being an egg isn't what it's cracked up to be.

But when I broke my way out, I couldn't find my family anywhere.

PEEP?

I looked all over the farm...

down by the cow pasture...

out by the duck pond... but I couldn't find them anywhere!

When I went to the pigsty, I met Pork Chop. He said he'd help me find them.

Frankie led Coop and Pork Chop to the henhouse.

Chickens aren't exactly known for their neat handwriting...

But something fell out of the envelope.

Coop, Frankie, and Pork Chop arrived at the marina, but it was too late. The cruise ship had already left.

Not wanting to lose any more time, the Squad raced to the submarine.

Back on track, the Coop Squad made their way out to sea.

I see it, Coop! I see the ship! We'll catch up to your family in no time.

The sub burbled through the water trying to catch up to the cruise ship. But Coop and his friends became distracted by their colorful surroundings.

The submarine puttered along when the Squad began to notice something happening. This part of the reef didn't look the same.

Coop looked ahead and saw a huge wad of tangled-up fishing net.

But that wasn't just a ball of fishing net. There was a turtle inside.

Coop and his crabby friends scuttled over to help the turtle escape the tangled mess.

Thanks. You all are turtley awesome.

How'd you get snarled up?

It was Captain Salty. He just chucked his old fishing net overboard again.

Who's Captain Salty?

21

Let me tell you about Captain Salty.

Captain Salty and his cat, Tuna, have fished from our coral reef for years.

At first, he just had a small boat and would take only a few fish—just what he needed.

Pretty soon, our coral reef started looking like this. Captain Salty would dump his trash and old nets, and the fish started to disappear.

Captain Salty got greedier and greedier. And Tuna got fatter and fatter.

When Coop got back to the sub, he told Frankie and Pork Chop about Captain Salty.

We have to do something to help save the reef.

What if we scare Captain Salty away?

Ooooh, sharks are pretty scary!

That's it! Coop, we'll go talk to the sharks and ask them for help.

SHARKS! I'm not going to talk to the sharks!

Don't be such a chicken. You can wear this so you'll blend in.

Captain Salty, encouraged by seeing the sharks, decided this was a perfect place to fish. Tuna was sent to check on the lobster traps.

Ready to save the reef, the Squad headed back over to Captain Salty's boat.

Pork Chop and his puffer pals had a plan of their own. Using puff power, they nudged the anchor off the coral.

Working together like a tornado, the fish swam circles around the fishing net, tangling it into a gigantic ball. Coop and the turtle hooked it back onto Captain Salty's line. He was in for a *reel* surprise.

Even with all their teamwork, the Squad had been outsmarted by Captain Salty, who was determined to stay.

But, while the others were carrying out the coral reef plan, Frankie had gone out for reinforcements.

With his giant size and strength, the whale shark effortlessly dragged the anchor and Captain Salty's tethered boat and awful claw over the reef wall to the bottom of the ocean. Captain Salty was no match for the biggest creature of the reef.

Without a boat,
Captain Salty and
Tuna would not
be back.

Meanwhile, Captain Salty and Tuna were looking at a rough situation.

Now he looks scared!

We nailed it this time!

Coop, Frankie, and Pork Chop looked at one another. They knew the right thing to do, even though it meant they wouldn't be able to catch up to the cruise ship.

When the sub dove under the ocean's surface to head back to shore, Captain Salty looked around.

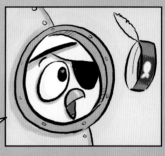

It looks terrible down here!

Hey, that looks familiar. Isn't that the same cat food you eat, Tuna?

Look! I used to have old ratty boots just like those. I chucked 'em overboard.

Who left all this garbage behind?

And then he realized it was him.

Frankie steered the submarine back to shore, passing along a different part of the reef.

This part of the reef is so colorful! There's no trash here.

Isn't it beautiful?

Hey, it looks like Tuna's made a friend!

Well, it looks like the reef was saved, but we'll never find the cruise ship now. It's too far away.

I'm sorry, Coop. We told you we'd find your family.

Did you say cruise ship? There was only one cruise ship that left today. I can tell you where it's heading.

Grateful for his newfound friends, the captain gave the Squad his compass to help guide them along the way.

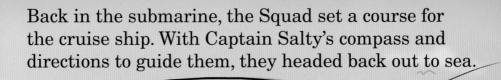

Back in the submarine, the Squad set a course for the cruise ship. With Captain Salty's compass and directions to guide them, they headed back out to sea.

Let's go find your family, Coop!

We'll meet them at the next port. We can do it, Squad!

You might be just a chicken, Coop, but you sure have a lot of cluck!

ONE YEAR LATER...
Captain Salty and Tuna returned to the reef. Now they run the most popular dive boat business in the area, taking tourists snorkeling and teaching them all about coral reefs. And, of course, Tuna loves visiting her new best friend.

How to Draw Coop!

Don't be a chicken! Grab a pencil, and let's get cracking!